© Naumann & Göbel Verlagsgesellschaft
in der VEMAG Verlags- und Medien AG, Cologne, Germany
All rights reserved
Illustrations by Anne Suess
Translated from the German by Joseph Swann
ISBN 3-625-20653-6

Fairytale Favourites

Illustrated by Anne Suess

NAUMANN & GÖBEL

Snow White

Once upon a time there was a queen who wanted
more than anything else to have a child. One
winter day she was sitting by a window sewing on
an embroidery-frame made of ebony, when she
pricked her finger with a needle and three drops
of blood fell onto the snow. "Ah," she sighed,
"if only I had a child white as the snow,
red as blood, and black as ebony."
In the course of the year she gave birth to a
daughter whose skin was white as the snow,
whose lips were red as blood, and whose hair
was black as ebony. For this reason she was called
Snow White. But the queen died when the child
was born, and the king took another wife.

The new queen was beautiful, but she was also proud and haughty and could not bear to be outdone in beauty. She had a magic mirror, and when she stood in front of it and asked, "Mirror, mirror on the wall, who is the fairest of us all?", the mirror answered, "My queen, you are the fairest in all the land." And the queen was happy, for the mirror had spoken the truth. Snow White, meanwhile, was growing up and becoming more beautiful by the day. Soon her beauty was so great that the queen felt uneasy. Standing in front of her mirror she asked, "Mirror, mirror on the wall, who is the fairest of us all?"
And the mirror answered, "My queen, you are the fairest here, but Snow White is a thousand times more fair."

From that moment on she hated the girl, and envy and jealousy
drove her so far that one day she gave an order to her hunter,
"Take the child into the forest and kill her. And as proof bring
me back her heart."

The hunter obeyed, but as he was about to kill Snow White she
began to cry and plead with him, "Dear hunter, please let me
live. I'll run far away into the forest and never return."

So the hunter took pity on her and thought, "Why should
I burden my conscience by killing this innocent child?
No, I'll let her escape." And as proof he brought the
queen back the heart of a deer he had killed. The queen
had it cooked and ate it, thinking it was Snow White's heart.

Poor Snow White, however, wandered about in the forest and soon felt lonely and afraid, trying to find her way through the dense undergrowth. The sharp stones hurt her feet and the sharp thorns tore her clothes. In the evening, worn out, she came to a cottage and went in.

Everything in the cottage was extremely small. On a low table seven places were set, each with a little vegetables and bread. There were seven small spoons, seven sets of knives and forks and seven tiny drinking cups. Against the wall stood seven small beds. As she was so hungry and thirsty, Snow White ate a little food from each plate and took a sip of drink from each cup. Then she lay down across several of the beds and fell immediately into a deep sleep.

During the night the seven dwarfs who lived in the cottage came home, each carrying a miner's lantern. By the light of the lanterns they saw immediately that someone had been there. The first of the dwarfs cried out, "Who has been sitting on my chair?" the second, "Who has been eating from my plate?" and the third, "Who has been eating my bread?" The fourth dwarf asked excitedly, "Who has been eating my vegetables?"

the fifth, "Who has been using my fork?" the sixth, "Who has been cutting with my knife?" and the seventh, "Who has been drinking from my cup?" Then they saw Snow White and exclaimed, "She is so beautiful. We won't disturb her." So the seven dwarfs lay down together in the remaining beds and the night passed.

In the morning, when Snow White saw the dwarfs, she was frightened at first. But they were very friendly to her, and when she had told them everything, they said, "Don't be afraid. You can stay with us and keep house for us."
"I'd do that with all my heart," Snow White replied – so she stayed with the dwarfs.
Every morning the little men went out into the mountains to mine for gold and ore, and by evening Snow White had cleaned the house, made the beds, done the washing and prepared a meal.

Now one day the queen stood again in front of her mirror and
asked, "Mirror, mirror on the wall, who is the fairest of us all?",
and the mirror answered, "My queen, you are the fairest here,
but over the hills where the seven dwarfs dwell, Snow White is
a thousand times more fair." Then the queen shook with rage
and began scheming again to kill Snow White. She disguised
herself as a pedlar and went to the dwarfs' cottage. "Fine goods
and cheap," she called. "What have you got to sell?" asked
Snow White. "Fine satin ribbons," the old woman cried, and the
girl opened the door and bought one. "Come here and let me
tie it for you," the old woman said. And she tied it so tight
around her that Snow White could no longer breathe and fell
down as if dead. "So much for your beauty now," the old
woman mocked and hurried away.

In the evening the dwarfs returned home from their work in the
mines. When they saw their beautiful Snow White lying there,
they thought she was dead. But then they saw the ribbon and
cut it through, and Snow White gradually came back to herself.
"The pedlar was none other than the wicked queen," they
exclaimed. "Take care, and don't buy anything from anyone
again."
When she got home, however, the wicked woman went up to her
mirror and asked, "Mirror, mirror on the wall, who is the fairest of
us all?" And the mirror answered, "My queen, you are the fairest
here, but over the hills where the seven dwarfs dwell, Snow White
is a thousand times more fair."

When she heard that, the queen's heart swelled with anger like a toad's belly and she plotted day and night to destroy Snow White. She spread poison on a golden comb, went again in disguise to the dwarfs' cottage and peddled her wares. Snow White looked out of the window. "I'm not allowed to buy anything," she said. "I'm not offering you anything to buy," the old woman replied. "Look, all I want to do is put this lovely golden comb in your hair." And she pressed the comb so hard into Snow White's hair that the poison began to work straight away and the girl fell down as if dead.

"There's your reward for being so very beautiful," the old woman cried, and hurried off as fast as she could.

And that is how the dwarfs found Snow White in the evening. But when they took the comb out of her hair she woke again. They warned her not to trust anyone at all any more, for they were very anxious about their beloved Snow White. But the queen, who by now had returned home, asked her magic mirror, "Mirror, mirror on the wall, who is the fairest of us all?" The mirror answered, "My queen, you are the fairest here, but over the hills where the seven dwarfs dwell, Snow White is a thousand times more fair."

When she heard that, the queen stamped her foot angrily and vanished into the room where she kept her poisons. Taking an apple, she poisoned half of it. Then she dressed up as a peasant woman and went out to the dwarfs' cottage to peddle her wares once more. Snow White called from the window, "I mustn't let anyone in. The dwarfs have forbidden me." "I just want to give you this lovely apple," the woman said coaxingly.

Snow White did not want to take it, but the old woman insisted. "Are you afraid it's poisoned? Look, I'll share it with you." And she gave Snow White the poisoned half, biting into the other half herself.

Snow White was so hungry for her half that she bit into it.
And hardly had she taken a bite when she fell down dead.
"Ha," the queen laughed, "this time you're really dead",
and went off home.
There she asked the mirror, "Mirror, mirror on the wall,
who is the fairest of us all?" And when the mirror answered,

"My queen, you are the fairest in all the land," her jealous
heart found rest at last.
This time the dwarfs could not wake Snow White, and as
they loved her so much and still wanted to look on her,
even now she was dead, they made her a coffin out of glass.
Weeping bitterly, they laid the lovely child in the coffin.

And for a long time Snow White lay there looking as if she was asleep. Then one day a king's son came into the forest and saw a young girl of astonishing beauty lying in the coffin. "Let me take Snow White," he begged, when the dwarfs had told him everything. "I'll give you whatever you want." "Snow White cannot be exchanged for gold," the dwarfs replied. "We'll not give you the coffin for all the money in the world."

When they saw, however, how deeply the prince loved
the king's beautiful daughter, their hearts melted and
they gave him the glass coffin.
The king's son ordered his servants to bear it away.
By chance one of them stumbled, and the piece of
apple was shaken by the jolt and fell out of Snow
White's throat. She immediately woke and sat up.
"Where am I?" she asked.

"You are with me," answered the king's son joyfully, and told her all that had happened. "I love you more than all the world," he said. "Come with me to my castle and be my wife."

And Snow White went with him, and their wedding was celebrated with great ceremony. As for the dwarfs, they were so happy that their beloved Snow White would now be queen that they sang and made music all night.

Cinderella

There was once a rich man whose wife became ill and died. Their only daughter sat weeping bitterly by her death-bed, and afterwards she went out to her mother's grave every day to think of her. Her father, however, married again, and his new wife brought two daughters into the house. A bad time began now for the stepdaughter, for the two sisters were fair and comely to look at, but dark and ugly in their hearts. They took away the girl's fine clothes and ordered her to do the heavy work in the kitchen. And then, because she always looked dusty and dirty, they mocked at her and called her Cinderella.

When one day the girl's father was setting out on a journey, he asked his two stepdaughters what he should bring them home. "Fine clothes," said the first. "Pearls and precious stones," the second. "And you, Cinderella," he asked, "what would you like?" "Father, the first branch that brushes your hat on your way home — break that off for me."

So he bought fine clothes, pearls and precious stones
for the two sisters, and when a branch of hazel brushed
against him on his way home, he broke it off and took it with
him. When he got home he gave his stepdaughters what they
had asked for, and to Cinderella he gave the branch from the
hazel bush. Cinderella thanked him, went to her mother's grave
and planted it, weeping so much that her tears watered the
branch on the grave. It grew into a fine tree, and every day
Cinderella went out to the tree and wept and prayed. And then a
white bird would fly down into the tree, and whenever Cinderella
wished for something, the bird would reach it down to her.

Then one day the king announced a
great festivity that was to last three days.
He invited all the beautiful girls in the land, for
his son was to choose a bride. The two sisters were
overjoyed. They called Cinderella and said, "Comb our hair,
clean our shoes and fasten our dresses. We're going to the ball
in the king's palace."
Cinderella did as she was told, but while she did so she wept,
because she would also have liked to go to the ball. She begged
her stepmother to let her, but she replied, "You Cinderella! You
want to go to the ball all covered with dust and dirt? You want
to go dancing when you've got no clothes or shoes?"

Cinderella, however, did not stop begging, so in the end her
stepmother said, "All right, I'll throw a basinful of lentils into the
cinders there for you. If you pick them out in two hours you can
go to the ball as well."

The girl ran out of the backdoor into the garden and called,
"Come, all you tame doves and turtle-doves! Come, all you birds
of the air! Help me pick out the lentils – the good into the pot,
the bad into your crop." Thereupon two great white doves flew in
through the kitchen window, followed by the turtle doves, and then

birds of every kind flocked in and settled by the cinders. Nodding their heads, the doves began – pick, pick, pick, pick – and the other birds followed suit – pick, pick, pick, pick – until all the good lentils were sorted into the bowl. It was hardly an hour before they had finished their work and flown away again. Then the girl took the bowl to her stepmother, happy in the thought that she could now go to the ball.

But the stepmother said, "No, Cinderella, you have no proper clothes and you can't dance. People will just laugh at you."

When the girl began to cry again,
however, she went on, "If you can pick two
basinfuls of lentils out of the cinders for me in
an hour, you can go."
– "She'll never manage that," she thought.
But when she had thrown the two bowls of lentils down among
the cinders, Cinderella ran out of the backdoor into the garden
and called, "Come, all you tame doves and turtle doves! Come,
all you birds of the air! Help me pick out the lentils – the good
into the pot, the bad into your crop."
Thereupon two great white doves flew in through the kitchen
window, followed by the turtle doves, and then birds of every
kind flocked in and settled by the cinders. Nodding their heads,
the doves began to pick and the other birds followed suit

until all the good lentils were sorted into the bowl. Scarcely half an hour had passed before they had finished their work and flown away again. Then the girl took the bowl to her stepmother, happy in the thought that she could now go to the ball. But the wicked woman said, "None of that is any use. You're not coming, because you have no proper clothes and you can't dance. You'd embarrass us." And saying that, she hurried off with her two proud daughters.

Now there was nobody left at home, so Cinderella went to her mother's grave beneath the hazel tree and called out, "Stir your branches, shake your leaves, O hazel tree! – Cast gold and silver over me!" And thereupon the bird reached down to her a dress made of gold and silver cloth, and slippers of silver silk.

Hurriedly Cinderella put on the dress and went to the ball. Her stepmother and stepsisters did not recognise her in the golden dress. But the king's son came up to her, took her hand and danced with her. He did not let go of her hand for a single moment, and when anyone came and asked her to dance, he said, "She is my partner."

So Cinderella danced till it was evening and she wanted to go home. But the king's son said, "I'll go with you and keep you company", for he wanted to see where this beautiful girl lived. Cinderella, however, managed to slip away from him.

When the stepmother
returned with her daughters,
Cinderella was sitting in the
kitchen wearing her grey
working dress. For she had
run straight to the hazel tree
in the churchyard and taken
off all her fine clothes. She
had laid them on the grave
and the bird had taken them
away again.

Next day, when the festivities started up again and her stepsisters had already left, Cinderella went to the hazel tree and said, "Stir your branches, shake your leaves, O hazel tree! – Cast gold and silver over me!" And thereupon the bird reached down to her a far finer dress than on the previous day. And when the girl appeared at the ball in that dress, everyone was amazed at her beauty. The king's son, however, had waited for her, and when she arrived he took her straight away by the hand and danced every dance with her. And when others came and asked her to dance, he said, "She is my partner." And in the evening, when Cinderella wanted to go home, he followed her to see which house she went into. But she slipped away from him unobserved.

When the others returned home, Cinderella was sitting as usual
in the kitchen, for she had taken her fine clothes back to the bird
in the hazel tree and put on her grey working dress again.
On the third day, when the wicked stepsisters had left, Cinderella
went once more to her mother's grave and spoke to the tree, "Stir
your branches, shake your leaves, O hazel tree! – Cast gold and
silver over me!" Now the bird reached down to her a dress that
shone with greater splendour than any she had yet worn, and
with it slippers of pure gold. The king's son danced with her
alone, and when anyone came and asked her to dance, he said,
"She is my partner."

When evening came, Cinderella wanted to leave, and the king's
son again wanted to accompany her. But she hurried away so fast
that he could not follow her. The king's son, however, had thought
up a trick and had had the staircase covered with pitch. And now,
when Cinderella ran off, the slipper from her left foot stuck fast
in the pitch. The king's son picked it up, and it was small and
delicate and made of the purest golden material. Next morning
he took the slipper to his father and said, "I shall take no other
wife but the one whose foot fits this golden shoe."
The two sisters rejoiced at this news, for they had fine feet.
The eldest took the shoe into her room to try it on – her
mother was there too.

But she could not get her big toe into the shoe,
for it was too small for her. Thereupon her mother
handed her a knife and said, "Cut the toe off! When you're queen,
you won't need to walk any more." So the girl cut her toe off and
forced her foot into the shoe. Biting her lip so as not to show the
pain, she went out to the king's son. He took her as his bride, sat
her upon his horse and rode off. But as they passed the grave the
two doves were sitting in the hazel tree and they called out,
"Cookety coo, cookety coo, there's blood in the shoe. The shoe is
too small. The true bride's at home, not here at all."

And when the king's son saw the blood pouring out of the shoe, he turned his horse and brought the false bride back home. He said she was not the right one, the other sister should try the shoe on. So the younger sister now went into her room, and her toes slipped into the shoe easily enough, but her heel was too big. Her mother handed her a knife and said, "Cut off a piece of the heel! When you're queen, you won't need to walk any more." So the girl cut off a piece of her heel and forced her foot into the shoe. Biting her lip so as not to show the pain, she went out to the king's son. He took her as his bride and rode off with her.

But as they passed the hazel tree the two
doves called out, "Cookety coo, cookety
coo, there's blood in the shoe. The shoe
is too small. The true bride's at home,
not here at all."
The king's son saw that the girl's stocking
was already stained red with blood, and
turning his horse he brought the false
bride back home. "She's not the right one
either," he said, "have you no other daughter?"
"No," the man replied, "only Cinderella, the
daughter of my first wife. She's a plain little
thing. She can't possibly be your future bride."

But the king's son insisted that he wanted to see Cinderella too. So the girl washed her hands and face and curtsied low before the king's son, who handed her the golden shoe. Then, sitting on a footstool, she took off her heavy wooden clog and slipped her foot into the shoe, which fitted as if hand-made.

When Cinderella stood and the king's son looked into her face,
he recognised the beautiful girl he had danced with at the ball
and cried, "That is my true bride."
The stepmother and the two sisters were appalled and went white
with rage. But he took Cinderella up onto his horse and rode off.

As they passed the hazel tree the two white doves called out, "Cookety coo, cookety coo, there's no blood in the shoe. The shoe's not too small. She's the true bride, riding there so tall." And having said this, they flew down and sat on Cinderella's shoulders, one to the right, the other to the left, and remained sitting there. On the day of the wedding to the king's son, the two sisters came and tried to flatter their way in and share Cinderella's joy.

As the bridal couple entered the church, the elder sister placed herself to the right and the younger to the left of the bride. Thereupon the doves pecked out an eye from each of them. Afterwards, as they left, the elder placed herself to the left and the younger to the right. Thereupon the doves pecked out the other eye. So for their falsehood and wickedness the two sisters were punished with lifelong blindness.

The Musicians of Bremen

There was once a man who had an old and faithful donkey. For many, many years the donkey had carried sacks to the mill and drawn the heavy cart, but now his strength was ebbing and with every day he was less able to work.

His master was vexed at this and considered how he might get rid of an animal whose only use was to eat the food he gave him. The donkey, who noticed that an ill wind was blowing, ran away.

Wondering how he could earn his living now,
he came to a decision – he would set out for
Bremen. There, the donkey thought to himself,
he could join the town band.

He trotted on for a while, sad and lonely, when he came upon an old brown hunting-dog that was panting and gasping as if worn out with running.

"What are you puffing like that for, Grappler?" the donkey asked.

"Ah!" said the dog, "I'm old and getting weaker by the day. And because I can't keep up with the hares at the hunt any more, my master wanted to beat me to death.

So I took my leave in a hurry – but how shall I earn my keep
now? I'll not find a new master at my age."
"I'll tell you something," the donkey confided, "I'm going to
Bremen to join the town band. Come along with me! I'll play
the lute and you can beat the drums."
The dog liked this idea, so they went on together.

They had not gone far when they saw a cat sitting in their way, her face like a three-day storm.

"Whatever's got into you, Whisker-Licker?" said the donkey. But the cat replied, "How can you make jokes when things are as bad as this?"

"Who's harming you, then?" asked the dog and donkey, looking sympathetically at the cat.

"I'm getting old and my teeth are going blunt, and because
I'd rather sit behind the stove dozing than chase mice, my
mistress wanted to drown me. I managed to escape, but now
I don't know what to do. Where shall I go?"
"Come with us to Bremen. There's no one better than you at
night music. You can join the town band too."
It seemed a good idea, so the cat joined them.

Soon afterwards the three of them came to a farm. The farmyard cockerel sat on the gate crowing for all he was worth. "Why are you crowing so loud, you'll waken the dead?" the donkey called out. "Huh!" the cockerel replied, "It's a scandalous ingratitude. Day in, day out I've woken the farmer and his folk, and always punctually. Now they're expecting guests on Sunday, and I'm going to be put in the pot. That's why I'm crowing – as long as I still can." "Rubbish, Redhead, you'll always find something better than death! You've got a fine voice. Why don't you come with us to Bremen. We're going to make music in the town." The cockerel liked this suggestion and went with them.

However, they couldn't reach Bremen in a single day, and that evening they came to a forest where they decided to spend the night. The donkey and the dog lay down under a big tree, the cat climbed onto a branch and the cockerel flew up into a treetop, where he felt safe. Before he went to sleep he saw a spark of light shining in the distance and called to his companions that there must be a house nearby. "In that case let's get up and go there," the donkey said, "for there's little comfort here."

So they made their way through the dark forest in the direction of the light. It grew brighter and brighter until they were standing in front of a well-lit house, from whose windows a warm glow shone out on the trees and bushes round about. The donkey, who was the tallest of them, went up to one of the windows and peered in.

"What can you see, Greycoat?" asked the cockerel.

"My friends," replied the donkey, "I can see a richly laid table with good food and drink in abundance – and robbers sitting round the table feasting." "How many robbers?" the companions asked. "I can see three," the donkey reported. "One of them looks like the leader, for he has a fierce moustache and wears a pointed hat with a feather. Another looks a nasty fellow, with a black shade over his right eye.

The third, with the long grey hair and the patched coat looks
a real simpleton."
"They're lucky sitting there in the warm," whinged the dog.
"That would be the place for us," crowed the cockerel.
"A full belly and a nap by the fire," purred the cat, a thrill of
pleasure running through her matted fur. And the animals
debated how they could best drive the robbers out of the house.

Finally they thought of a way. The donkey would stretch his front hoofs up to the window sill, the dog would then jump on the donkey's back, the cat would climb onto the dog and the cockerel would fly up and sit on the cat's head. So they arranged themselves in this way, and when that was done a sign was given, and they all began at the same moment to make music.

The donkey brayed for all he was worth, the dog barked furiously, the cat wailed pitifully enough to freeze your blood and the cockerel crowed shrilly. Then they burst through the window into the room, shattering the glass so that it fell tinkling to the floor.

The robbers were so startled by the din that they jumped out of their chairs, sending them flying and spilling the wine. They thought a fearful demon had come in through the window and fled terrified into the forest. As the house was now empty, the four companions sat down at the table and ate their fill, enjoying whatever the robbers had left.

The donkey ate carrots and grapes, the dog fed on sausages and ham. The cat found fresh fish to still her hunger, and the cockerel feasted on breadcrumbs and grain. They ate as if they had to starve for the next four weeks, for they had no idea how long their good life might last.

After the sumptuous meal they looked for a place to sleep, each of them according to their nature and sense of ease. The donkey lay down on the dunghill, the dog behind the door, the cat by the warm stove and the cockerel perched high on a wooden beam. When the robbers saw from a distance that there was no light burning in the house any more, their leader spoke "We shouldn't have let ourselves be frightened like that," he said, and ordered the simpleton to go and inspect the house. The robber tiptoed into the kitchen to light a lamp.

Mistaking the cat's gleaming eyes for coals, he held a match to them. But the cat was not in a playful mood. She leapt into the robber's face, spat, scratched and snarled. Shocked out of his wits, he ran to the door. But the dog, lying behind the door, sprang up and bit him in the leg. The donkey kicked him as he was running past the dunghill and, perched on his beam, the cockerel chanted, "Cock-a-doodle-do, cock-a-doodle-do."

The robber ran as fast as he could back to his leader and said, "The devil himself has got into our house, and brought all sorts of dreadful companions with him. There's a witch sitting by the stove. She shot sparks at me with her glowing eyes, then snarled spitefully at me and scratched my face with her long nails. There's a strong man standing by the door holding a knife – he stabbed me in the leg with it. And there's a black monster lying out in the yard. It beat me so hard with its club

that I only just escaped. And
up on the roof there's a judge
calling, 'Bring me out the rogue,
bring me out the rogue!' I fled as fast as
I could." From that moment on, the robbers did not
dare enter the house again. But the four musicians of Bremen
were so happy there that they never wanted to leave.

The Nutcracker

Once upon a time there was a family that celebrated
Christmas Eve in the way that many Christians do all over
the world. Round the shimmering, brightly decorated
Christmas tree with its candles burning sat mother and
father, grandmother and grandfather, uncles and aunts
and, of course, the children. First they all sang together,
then father read the Christmas story, and finally came
what everyone had been longing for – the presents.

The children were allowed to stay up longer than on any
other day in the year so that they could play with their
presents. But the time came when they were tired too,
and began to yawn and rub their eyes. Mother thought
it was high time the children went to sleep, and sent
them off to bed.

Clara took all her presents with her, for she could not
bear parting from them. She wanted her new teddy, the
beautiful doll, the storybook, the silver box of spiced
shortbread, the tray of sweets and the smart nutcracker
soldier all to be there next morning when she woke up.
She was particularly fascinated by the nutcracker –
a wooden figure in red and blue tunic, white trousers
and black boots, with gleaming gold buttons and a
long sabre. His dark brown moustache curled boldly
upwards and his blue eyes shone brightly.

With her new teddy under her arm, Clara climbed into bed. Spread out on the floor, the presents glistened in the moonlight that shone softly in through the window. All of a sudden it seemed to Clara that the nutcracker had moved. And yes! – everywhere little figures were flitting busily around. A band of mice had set to work on the sweets and were paying particular attention to the shortbread. High above them on the rocking chair stood the mouse king, richly clad in golden crown and sceptre, encouraging his subjects to eat their fill.

And then something happened that was quite impossible to explain. One, two, three, four, five other nutcrackers appeared and began to swing their sabres. With sparkling eyes and clenched teeth they set about the mice, determined to drive those thieving visitors away. But it was only when Clara, who must have seemed to them a giant, got out of bed, that the mouse king gave a shrill whistle and all his people vanished. What a good thing she had come to the rescue! Otherwise the mice might have gnawed the nutcrackers to pieces and turned them into a heap of sawdust with their sharp teeth.

The nutcracker wanted to thank Clara for saving him and his companions, so when the mice had finally fled, he invited her to go with him on a journey to the kingdom of his future bride, the sugar plum fairy.

Clara was thrilled at the idea, and after she had fetched her teddy, the nutcracker took her by the hand and the journey began. From somewhere she heard music playing, and the whole company began to move to its melody. Clara felt as if she was not walking on the ground any more, but on clouds sprinkled with sparkling stars.

While they were still some way off, Clara caught sight of a candy-pink staircase which led, she supposed, to the fairy's magic castle. And then something wonderful happened again.

As Clara and the nutcrackers passed through the open gates of the castle, the wooden figures were transformed into men of flesh and blood. Clara was amazed to see her own nutcracker turn before her eyes into a real prince. With open arms the young man ran towards a most beautiful woman and they embraced joyfully — the sugar plum princess and the prince, who many years ago had been turned by a wicked magician into a wooden nutcracker along with all his servants and followers. Full of gratitude the prince told the entire company that they owed their salvation to Clara's help.

The sugar plum fairy was so delighted at the return of her beloved
that she immediately commanded a great feast to be made. Soon
a troupe of Cossacks in high fur caps and tall boots stormed into
the banqueting hall and performed their spirited dance.
Clara watched excitedly as they leapt high into the air, kicking
out their legs and shouting their wild cries.

After this performance, the sugar plum fairy gave a sign with her hand and two Arabs in brilliant white robes came in, bearing a tray of richly scented coffee. Once again Clara heard music playing, but this time it was very different from the furious Cossack chants. And when two graceful women began to dance in the eastern manner, their veils wafting magically through the air, she seemed to be transported into a fairytale from the *Arabian Nights*.

"My kingdom is a peaceful corner of the earth," said the sugar plum fairy. "People of every colour, with very different habits and customs, live happily together. This variety makes our life here interesting."

A gong sounded and a Chinese man and woman
appeared, dressed in wonderful silk kimonos, and served tea
– the national drink of China – in delicate porcelain cups.
The princess thanked them, joining her hands together and
gently bowing her head, and Clara did the same. Thereupon
the Chinese tea-bearers withdrew with small, elegant steps.

After a short pause the sugar plum fairy and her prince took
Clara between them and strolled through the vast hall.
The little girl thought she was dreaming when she discovered
all around her delicious sweets and biscuits. In an alcove stood
a three-tiered wedding cake decorated with marzipan roses
and topped by two icing-sugar doves.

Now the princess touched some sticks of candy with her magic wand, turning them instantly into jolly wooden pipes. Big and small, fat and thin, they joined hands in a merry jig, playing a medley of notes, high and low, gentle and lively, to whose rhythm they gracefully danced.

The feast in the sugar castle now reached
its high point. The prince and princess took
the floor in a dance of honour, while everyone
looked happily on – Clara with her teddy, the two Arabs in their
white robes, the elegant women dancers, the gracious Chinese
man with his wife and little boy, and the pipes, which till a
moment ago had been sticks of candy. Scarcely had the dance
ended when the music began again, and all the spectators now
joined the couple in a happy waltz. From roses and lilac,
bluebells and sunflowers and every blossom that adorned the
room came a sweet, heady scent.

The prince and princess had found each other again, and little Clara dreamed on of her magic journey to the land of the sugar plum fairy, until – well until the first rays of the sun woke her on Christmas morning. She looked sleepily round and saw all her presents lying just where she had left them the night before. Not even the spiced shortbread showed any marks of nibbling teeth. But from that night on, Clara kept a special place in her heart for the nutcracker.

Peter and the Wolf

Far away from the town was a corner of the countryside which counted more hares and foxes than people. There, in a broad, sweeping meadow at the edge of the forest, Peter's grandfather had many years ago built himself a little thatched cottage, where he lived with a duck and a cat called Tiger.

Every year Peter spent his holidays at his grandfather's house. One morning he opened the garden gate and ran out into the meadow. He was happy to be in the country again, and began to watch a little bird that was flying round him twittering gaily. He did not notice that the duck had followed him out onto the meadow.

The duck waddled straight down to the pond by the great oak
tree and was enjoying a cool, refreshing morning dip. Preening its
glossy plumage, it pecked now at this, now at that tuft of feathers,
uttering every so often a satisfied "Quack, quack!"
Curious to see what was going on, the little bird flew up.

"What sort of a bird do you call yourself if you can't fly?"
it called cheekily. "What sort of a bird do you call yourself
if you can't swim?" replied the duck.
Meanwhile Peter lay happily in the grass, listening to the pair
of them as they argued loudly. Suddenly Tiger the cat came
creeping across the meadow. At the sight of the bird its mouth
began to water.

But Peter didn't want the cat to catch the little bird, so he clapped his hands, and quick as lightning the bird flew up into the oak tree. The duck, too, was startled and splashed its way quacking excitedly out of the pond. As for the cat, it began to circle the tree, wondering if it was worth climbing all the way up. "Because when I get there the bird will already have flown away," it reflected.

Peter was relieved to see the bird gazing boldly down at the cat again. It seemed to have lost its fear altogether. Just then he noticed his grandfather coming towards him. The old man spoke severely, "Peter, you left the garden gate open. You know how dangerous that is. The wolf might come out of the forest and get into our garden."

But Peter did not want to listen to such talk. On the contrary, he thought meeting a wolf would be an exciting adventure. The old man realised this and, taking Peter by the hand, led him without more ado back into the garden and shut the gate. What happened next was something Peter would never forget.

Although he could not see what was going on at the other side
of the high garden wall, he heard the furious squawking of the
duck and the terrified miaowing of the cat. In his haste, Peter's
grandfather had left the two animals out on the meadow. Peter
was sure now that the wolf had arrived.

Before long it discovered the cat, sitting trembling on a branch
above its head. And on another branch just opposite perched the
little bird, staring with equal terror at the wolf pacing menacingly
below. Peter, who had managed to get up onto the garden gate,
felt his skin turn to gooseflesh at the sight of the three creatures.

And it had. Bounding out of the forest with powerful steps, the savage grey creature had set about chasing the duck, which ran before it now, screeching in mortal fear. The wolf came closer … and closer … and … snap! In a single gulp it had swallowed the duck alive. Then it looked greedily round the meadow, for that little snack had not yet satisfied its hunger.

He felt sorry for the cat and the little bird. But being a good-natured boy, he soon overcame his fear and began to consider how he could trick the hungry wolf and rescue the cat and the bird. He had an idea …

Quickly running into the house he found a strong rope, wound it round his shoulder and jumped up onto the garden wall. From there he climbed into the tree where the cat and the bird were perched, petrified with fear.

He whispered his plan to the two terrified animals. The cat regained enough courage to jump down to the safety of the grandfather's garden. Then Peter spoke in a gentle voice to the bird, "Fly down and flutter round the wolf's head, but make sure it doesn't catch you."

The little bird plucked up its courage and flew in dizzying circles round the wolf's open jaws, maddening it with rage.

The cheekiness of the bird whipped the wolf into a fury. Snarling, it bared its teeth and leapt from right to left in its desire to snap up the little rascal. But in vain! The bird flitted again and again out of range, and in its anger the wolf did not notice that Peter was gently lowering a noose, which he skilfully dropped over the wolf's tail. Quick as lightning he pulled the rope tight and the robber was caught.

When the wolf saw that it was trapped, it began to jump wildly
in every direction in an effort to break loose. But escape was
impossible, for Peter had wisely tied the other end of the rope
round a stout branch.

The higher the wolf leapt the more firmly it caught itself in the rope. But still it fought bitterly for freedom. Then, seeing that the situation was hopeless, it began howling plaintively. Peter's grandfather, who was a little deaf, had not noticed what was going on at all, so Peter was quite relieved when two hunters appeared on the scene.

They had come upon the wolf's tracks in the forest and followed them. They could scarcely believe their eyes when they saw the wolf so close to the grandfather's house. They raised their guns to their shoulders and were just about to shoot, and finally get rid of the dangerous creature, when Peter called down from the tree, "Stop! Stop! Don't shoot! The wolf is caught and can't harm anyone any more."

The hunters cautiously approached the wolf. One of them took the rope that held its tail, while the other caught its mouth firmly and bound it up quickly so that it could no longer bite. Only when this was done did Peter climb down from the safety of the tree.

Generously he begged the hunters to take the wolf to the zoo – he did not want it to be shot. And because he had been so brave, the hunters were willing to agree with his suggestion.

Meanwhile Peter's grandfather had come out of the cottage carrying the cat on his arm. He could not believe his eyes when he saw Peter and the two hunters with the wolf roped between them. He thought he must be dreaming. And above them flew the little bird, chirping its tale of how Peter had captured the wolf. What a brave deed it was! So in a triumphal procession they accompanied the wolf to the zoo, where it lived happily to the end of its days.

The Russian composer Sergei Prokofiev had also heard the tale
of Peter and the Wolf, and he liked it so much that in 1936 he
turned it into a musical play for children.
He gave each figure in the story a different instrument. The deep,
echoing sound of the horn takes the part of the great grey wolf.
The clarinet plays the cat, slinking about on velvet paws,
miaowing sometimes with fear, sometimes with contentment.
And the oboe quacks like a duck.

With its clear, high notes the flute plays the role of the jolly little bird, chirping gaily. And we recognise Peter from a special tune played on the violins. His grandfather's slow, steady steps are given by the solemn bassoon, and the arrival of the hunters is announced with a rolling beat of drums. So if you listen carefully you'll seem to hear what the people and the animals in the fairytale are doing, and what they're saying too. And you'll get to know the instruments of the orchestra as well.
A wonderful adventure!

Hansel and Gretel

Once upon a time there was a poor woodcutter who lived with his wife and two children at the edge of a great forest. The boy's name was Hansel and the girl's was Gretel.

They were very poor, and as great
hardship had spread over the land
their father could not earn enough
for their daily bread. "What shall we
do?" he asked his wife. "We can't
feed the children any more."

"Listen," she answered, "tomorrow morning at daybreak we'll go out with the children into the forest, and we'll leave them in the thickest part of the wood. They won't be able to find their way home, and we'll be rid of them." "No," said the man, "I won't do that!" But his wife gave him no peace till he agreed.

The children had not been able to sleep for hunger and they heard everything their parents said. Gretel started to cry bitterly, but Hansel said, "Don't cry, Gretel. I have a plan."

When his parents had gone to sleep he crept out of the house. In the bright moonlight he filled his pockets with white pebbles, slipped back into the house and got back into bed. At daybreak the woman woke the children. "Get up," she said, "we're going out into the forest to gather wood." She gave each of them a piece of bread for their lunch and they set off into the forest. Hansel went last so that he could drop pebbles behind him all along the way without being noticed.

When they got to the middle of the forest their father said, "Go and collect some wood, I want to light a fire." Hansel and Gretel gathered brushwood and soon a bright fire was burning. "Lie down by the fire, children, and have a rest," his wife told them, "we're going further into the forest to cut wood. In the evening we'll come and fetch you." So Hansel and Gretel sat down by the fire. At midday they ate their bread, then evening came and they grew weary. Shutting their eyes, they fell into a deep sleep from which they only awoke when it was already dark.

Gretel began to cry, but Hansel consoled her. "We'll find our way back," he said, and when the moon had risen he took his sister by the hand and they followed the path marked out by the pebbles, which shone brightly in the moonlight. They walked all night, and by morning had arrived back at their father's house. The woman opened to them when they knocked, and when she saw that it was Hansel and Gretel she scolded them, "You naughty children, why have you been sleeping so long in the wood?" But their father was happy that the children were home again.

Not long afterwards, however, they heard his wife say, "We have only half a loaf of bread left in the house. The children must go. We'll have to take them even deeper into the forest, so that they won't be able to find their way back."

The man was sad in his heart at this, but in the end he yielded. The children had listened to this conversation too, and when his parents had gone to sleep, Hansel wanted to go out and collect pebbles again, but he found the doors locked. He spoke soothingly to his sister, "Don't cry, Gretel, we'll think of something."

Early in the morning the woodcutter's wife gave the children a crust of bread and then they set off. Hansel walked behind again, and every now and then he dropped a few crumbs along the way, to help them find their way home.

The woman led them deep into the forest, to a part where they
had never been before. Again they lit a fire, and again she said,
"Lie down, children, and sleep a bit. We're going further into the
forest to cut wood. In the evening we'll come and fetch you."
When midday came, Gretel shared her bread with Hansel,
who had used his for the crumbs he had strewn along the way.
Then the children fell asleep, but no one fetched them and
when they awoke it was already dark. Hansel consoled his sister,
"Wait until the moon rises. Then we'll see the breadcrumbs and
find our way home."
When the moon rose they set out, but they found no breadcrumbs
– the birds had eaten them all. Hansel said to Gretel,
"Don't worry, we'll find the way." But they didn't.

They walked all night and the next day too, from morning till evening, but they were still inside the forest. They were sad and hungry, for they had only eaten a few berries which they found in the wood. When they grew so tired that their legs would no longer carry them, they lay down under a tree and went to sleep.

When morning came it was three days since they had
left their father's house. They set off again and wandered
on through the forest. Then they noticed a small snow-
white bird flying in front of them as if it wanted to show
them the way. They followed it until they came to a little
house that was made entirely of cake and shortbread,
with windows of sugar candy.

"Let's eat till we're full," Hansel cried, pulling down a piece of the roof. Gretel broke off a piece of window-pane and started to nibble at it. It tasted delicious. Suddenly a voice called from inside the house,

"Nibble, nibble, mouse,
who's nibbling at my house?"

The children answered,

> "The wind so wild,
> the heavenly child!"

and calmly went on eating. With that, the door opened
and an ancient woman came out, leaning on a stick.
Hansel and Gretel were so startled that they dropped
everything they were holding.

The old woman shook her head and spoke, "Oh, you little darlings, come in and stay with me for a while. I won't do you any harm" – and saying this she led them into the house. Good food was served – milk and pancakes with sugar, apples and nuts. Then two comfortable beds were prepared. Hansel and Gretel lay down in them and thought themselves in heaven.

But that was not the end of it with the old woman, for she was an evil and terrible witch who lured children into her shortbread house and ate them, once she had fattened them up. That was what she intended to do with Hansel and Gretel.

She got up early in the morning before the children woke, and seeing them so sweetly lying there she murmured, "That will be a tasty meal." Then she picked Hansel up, carried him out to a little hut and locked him in. Shaking Gretel awake, she commanded her, "Get up, fetch water and cook something nice for your brother. He's sitting outside in the hut and must be fattened up. When he's ready I'll eat him." Gretel wept bitterly, but she had to do what the witch demanded. Poor Hansel was fed on the best of everything and Gretel had no proper food at all. Every morning the old woman hobbled to the hut and called, "Hansel, hold out your finger so that I can feel whether you'll soon be fat enough."

But Hansel held out a small bone that Gretel had secretly given him, and as the old woman had poor eyesight she thought it was Hansel's finger. She was surprised that he was not growing any fatter, and after four weeks she began to get impatient. "Gretel, come here," she ordered, "go and fetch water for the pot. Whether Hansel's fat or thin, he'll be killed and cooked tomorrow." How the poor girl sobbed and wept! Early next morning she had to hang the great cauldron full of water and light the fire beneath it. Then the old woman said, "First we'll do the baking. I've already started heating the oven. Climb inside and see if it's hot enough to put the bread in."

She wanted to shut the oven door once Gretel was inside and eat her, too, when she was nicely baked. But Gretel realised that the old witch meant no good and said, "I don't know how to do that. How can I get in? Show me, then I'll do it." "Silly goose," scolded the witch, "the door's big enough, you can see that. I could get in myself." Saying this, she put her own head inside the oven. Gretel immediately gave her a push that sent her tumbling in and bolted the iron door tight shut. "Aaaagh!" the witch began to wail and howl most horribly, but Gretel ran off and the old woman was burnt to a cinder.

Hurrying to the hut, Gretel unlocked the door and called out, "Hansel, we're free. The witch is dead." Overjoyed, the two children fell into each other's arms. In the same moment there was a great cracking noise and the oven collapsed, and with it the whole house. Out of the ruins came children who had been trapped by the wicked witch before. No longer needing to fear anything, they searched through the remains of the house, and

in every corner they found chests of gold and precious stones from which they filled their pockets to overflowing.

Then they left, for they wanted to escape from the witch's forest as fast as they could. After some hours' journey they came to a wide stretch of water. "We can't get across," said Hansel, "for I can see neither bridge nor stepping stones." But a beautiful swan came floating by and they called out to it, "Oh gentle swan, please bear us on." Bowing its head, the swan glided up to them and carried the children, one after the other, to the opposite bank.

Hansel and Gretel walked on for a while, and
gradually the wood became more familiar to them,
until finally in the distance they saw their father's house.
Then they began to run, burst in through the doorway and
fell into their father's arms.

The poor man had not had a single happy moment since he had left his children in the wood. Meanwhile, however, his selfish wife had died and he had married again. Gretel shook out her apron till the whole cottage sparkled with gold and precious stones. All their cares had an end, and they lived happily together for the rest of their lives.